Parents and Caregivers,

Stone Arch Readers are designed to provide enjoyable reading experiences, as well as opportunities to develop vocabulary, literacy skills, and comprehension. Here are a few ways to support your beginning reader:

- Talk with your child about the ideas addressed in the story.

- Discuss each illustration, mentioning the characters, where they are, and what they are doing.

- Read with expression, pointing to each word. You may want to read the whole story through and then revisit parts of the story to ensure that the meanings of words or phrases are understood.

- Talk about why the character did what he or she did and what your child would do in that situation.

- Help your child connect with characters and events in the story.

Remember, reading with your child should be fun, not forced. Each moment spent reading with your child is a priceless investment in his or her literacy life.

Gail Saunders-Smith, Ph.D.

Stone Arch Readers

are published by Stone Arch Books
a Capstone Imprint
1710 Roe Crest Drive
North Mankato, Minnesota 56003
www.capstonepub.com

Library of Congress Cataloging-in-Publication Data
Yasuda, Anita.
The crazy clues / by Anita Yasuda ; illustrated by Steve Harpster.
p. cm. -- (Stone Arch readers: Dino detectives)
Summary: Dot the Diplodocus is puzzled by the strange behavior of her family and friends, but when she investigates she finds a trail of popcorn that leads her to an answer.
ISBN 978-1-4342-5971-4 (library binding) -- ISBN 978-1-4342-6200-4 (pbk.)
1. Dinosaurs--Juvenile fiction. 2. Parties--Juvenile fiction. 3. Best friends--Juvenile fiction. [1. Dinosaurs--Fiction. 2. Parties--Fiction. 3. Best friends--Fiction. 4. Friendship--Fiction. 5. Mystery and detective stories.]
I. Harpster, Steve, ill. II. Title.
PZ7.Y2124Cr 2013
813.6--dc23   2012046962

Reading Consultants:
Gail Saunders-Smith, Ph.D
Melinda Melton Crow, M.Ed
Laura K. Holland, Media Specialist

Designer: Russell Griesmer

Printed in China by Nordica.
0314/CA21400182
022014
007226NORDF13

by **Anita Yasuda**
illustrated by **Steve Harpster**

STONE ARCH BOOKS
a capstone imprint

Meet the Dino Detectives!

Dot the Diplodocus

Sara the Triceratops

Cory the Corythosaurus

Ty the T. rex

Dot is excited. It is her last day
of swim lessons.

She thinks she finally passed
level one.

Dot sees her mom baking in the kitchen.

"Strange. Mom never bakes,"
Dot whispers to Teddy.

Dot hears her dad on the phone
talking about balloons.

"Strange. Dad never talks on the phone," Dot whispers to Teddy.

Dot sees her brother mowing
the lawn.

"Strange. Dex never mows,"
Dot whispers to Teddy.

Dot calls her friends. Nobody is home.

"Strange. All of my friends are gone," she whispers to Teddy.

"What a mystery!" she says
to Teddy. "I need to make a list
of clues."

"These are some crazy clues!"
she says.

"You are going to be late for swim lessons," her mom says.

"I'm just leaving," Dot says.
"Bye, Mom!"

"Have fun," her mom says.

Dot zooms off on her bike with
Teddy in the basket.

"We will have to solve this
mystery later," Dot says to Teddy.

After swim lessons, Dot bikes
home. Nobody is there.

"Where is everyone?" she asks
Teddy. "I have some big news."

Dot gets her list of clues. Then she sees a trail of popcorn.

She follows the trail to the backyard.

"Surprise!" everyone yells.

"It's not my birthday," says Dot.

"But you finally passed level one," says her mom.

"How did you know my big
news?" Dot asks.

"Your teacher called last night," her dad says.

"Way to go, Dot!" her friends cheer.

STORY WORDS

lessons	kitchen	mystery
level	strange	solved

Total Word Count: 250